O9-ABF-457

little brothers
& little sisters

little brothers
& little sisters

monica arnaldo

Owlkids Books

In nearly every
neighborhood of
almost every town,

you will find
little brothers and
little sisters,

all longing for
the same few things…

A turn at the wheel.

A promotion.

The secret password.

A place on the team.

The good spot.

Invisibility.

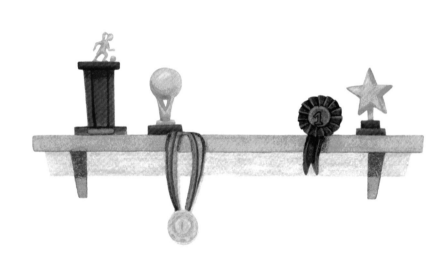

A second chance.

A helping hand.

A bodyguard.

A partner in crime.

An expert teacher.

A fearless leader.

A best friend.

To my big brother, Jose. Thanks for showing me the ropes. —M.A.

Owlkids Books acknowledges the financial support of the Canada Council for the Arts, the Ontario Arts Council, the Government of Canada through the Canada Book Fund (CBF) and the Government of Ontario through the Ontario Media Development Corporation's Book Initiative for our publishing activities.

Published in Canada by
Owlkids Books Inc.
10 Lower Spadina Avenue
Toronto, ON M5V 2Z2

Published in the United States by
Owlkids Books Inc.
1700 Fourth Street
Berkeley, CA 94710

Library and Archives Canada Cataloguing in Publication

Arnaldo, Monica, author, illustrator
        Little brothers & little sisters / [written and illustrated by] Monica Arnaldo.

ISBN 978-1-77147-295-1 (hardcover)

        I. Title. II. Title: Little brothers and little sisters.

PS8601.R6453L58 2018   jC813'.6   C2017-904413-3

Library of Congress Control Number: 2017945882

Edited by: Debbie Rogosin and Karen Li
Designed by: Danielle Arbour

Manufactured in Shenzhen, China, in October 2017, by C&C Joint Printing Co.
Job #HR4255

A   B   C   D   E   F

Publisher of Chirp, chickaDEE and OWL
www.owlkidsbooks.com | Owlkids Books is a division of Bayard CANADA